For Alfie, with love ~ H. W.
For Becky & Mike ~ I. A.

Published in 2005 by Simply Read Books
www.simplyreadbooks.com

Cataloguing in Publication Data

Ward, Helen, 1962-
  The Boat / Helen Ward ; illustrated by Ian Andrew.

ISBN 1-894965-18-3

  I.Andrew, Ian P., 1962- II. Title.

PZ7.W24Bo2005   823'.914   C2004-905677-8

First published in the UK by Templar Publishing.

Color tinting by Jonathan Lambert
Designed by Mike Jolley
Edited by A.J.Wood

The pictures in this book were rendered in pencil on paper.

10 9 8 7 6 5 4 3 2 1

Printed in Hong Kong

BOAT
The

Helen Ward & Ian Andrew

SIMPLY READ BOOKS

ON A HILL
AMONG HILLS
LIVED ONE OLD MAN.

For as long as anyone could remember he had shared his home
with many strange animals.

They were creatures that had been hurt or abandoned, neglected
or forgotten, and he cared for each one with love.

All his grumpiness was saved for another kind of creature,
the noisiest, messiest, most inconsiderate kind he knew…

They lived in a village on another hill.

They were scared of the grumpy old man and his wild collection of animals and everyone was happy with the distance between them.

Everyone, except for one young boy.
He had watched from a distance as the old man
took his creatures wandering through the fields.
He heard the tenderness in his voice and saw there
was nothing to be frightened of.

Why couldn't the villagers see it, too?

THEN, ONE EVENING, IT BEGAN TO RAIN.

Over the hills and under the sky, the wind sent clouds the color of bruises, and the first fat drops began to fall.

Trickles tipped caterpillars
  off their twigs, and turned to torrents.
  Swollen streams snatched the nests from under
  ducks and forced moles from their earth fortresses.

THE BOY
LOOKED OUT
THROUGH THE RAIN.

He watched as it fed and overfilled every stream, until the river between the hills spilled across the land… and became a sea… and turned the old man's hill into an island.

Over the water the boy could see frightened animals and he too grew afraid of what would happen to them if the water kept rising…

It seemed there was nothing he could do.
From the rising shore he looked out towards the old man's island, which grew smaller every hour.

Through the wind and the rain came the bellowing and bleating of beasts.

And then it happened.
Through the gloom and driving rain,

A BOAT APPEARED.

Twisting towards the shore, it beached close by, hollow and empty. He waded in and caught it before it could float away.

The boy rowed the boat across the rising water.
There was no welcome.

The old man shouted and bellowed louder
than his animals.
"Go away!" he yelled.
"We don't need your help! Go away!"
The old circus lion roared in fear,
but the boy knew it was not just the
animals who were frightened.

Quickly, he loaded the nearest creatures
into the boat and rowed them back
to a safer shore.

When he returned,
the old man had grown silent, watching.

Far away, on the shore beneath the village, people had gathered.
They had opened their sheds and barns to provide shelter for the old
man's creatures. They had brought blankets and baskets in case they were
needed. Tenderly, they helped the wet, bedraggled animals ashore.

THIS TIME the old man did not shout
as the boy filled the boat with
its precious cargo.

AGAIN
THE BOY
ROWED BACK
ACROSS THE SEA,
and this time the villagers were waiting.

Tin baths and barrels
that once held water in now kept water out,
knotted together into a makeshift raft
so more creatures could
be rescued.

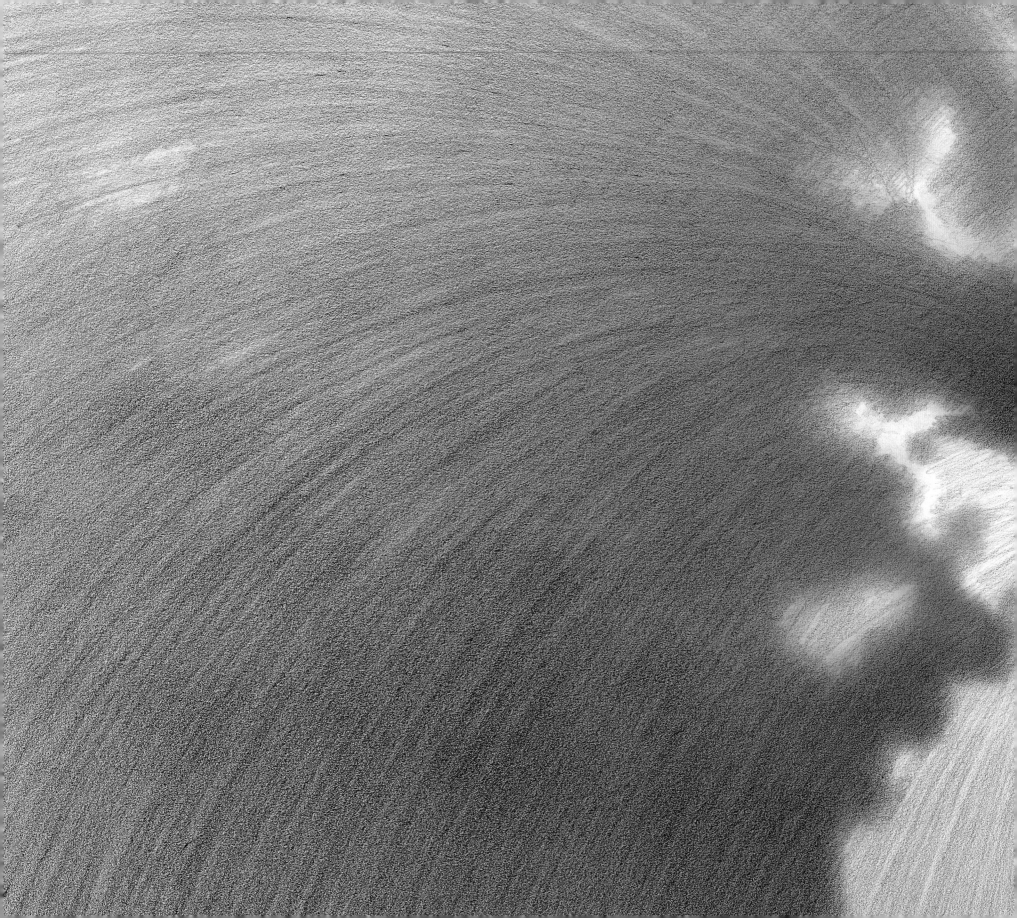

From his flooded fortress the old man watched
as the boy set out once more towards him.

He saw the raft coming to rescue his animals
from their shrinking home.

"Come on!" called the boy to the old man,
    "It's all right! Come on! There's no need to be frightened."

AND FINALLY
HE CAME.

TOGETHER, BOY AND MAN
loaded the raft with the last
of the animals, the biggest
beasts of the menagerie,
and set out, with those animals
that could swim following behind.

With the last of their strength,
they rowed for home as the
island sank beneath the waters.

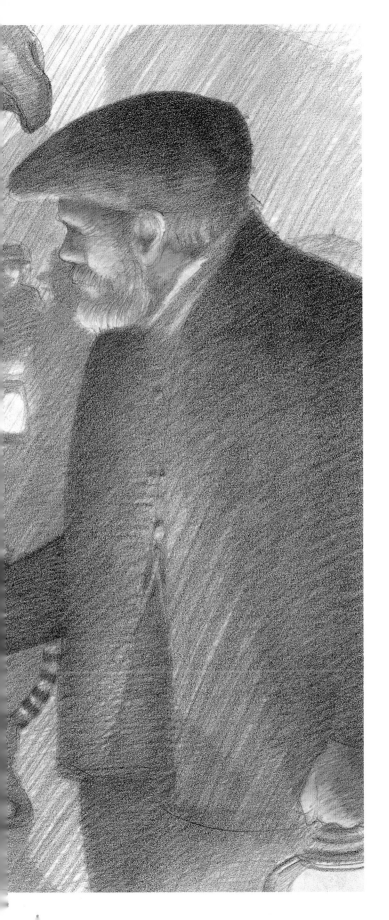

THE PEOPLE STARED

uneasily at the old man. Nervously,
the old man looked at the people.
In every home, his creatures had been
given shelter. There was a place for each
and every one and for the old man too.

"Thank you," he said smiling,
his tears lost in the rain.
They were the only two words that
were needed.

The villagers came forward to greet him…

AND THE RAIN
BEGAN
TO
END.